Carnival of the Animals

by Saint-Saëns

Commentary by

Barrie Carson Turner

Illustrations by

Sue Williams

Henry Holt and Company   •   New York

For Wilfred and Edwin Wallis —S. W.

Henry Holt and Company, LLC
Publishers since 1866
175 Fifth Avenue
New York, New York 10010
mackids.com

Henry Holt® is a registered
trademark of Henry Holt and Company, LLC.
Text copyright © 1998 by Macmillan Children's Books
Illustrations copyright © 1998 by Sue Williams
All rights reserved.
First published in the United States in 1999 by
Henry Holt and Company
Originally published in the United Kingdom in 1998
by Macmillan Children's Books

Library of Congress Catalog Card Number: 98-074161

ISBN 978-0-8050-6180-2

First American Edition—1999
Printed in Malaysia by Tien Wah Press (Pte) Ltd.

19   20   18

Contents

Saint-Saëns's Carnival 8

Orchestra for the Carnival 10

String Instruments 12

Woodwind Instruments 14

Xylophone, Glockenspiel, and Piano 16

Royal March of the Lion 19

Hens and Roosters 21

Mules 23

Tortoises 25

The Elephant 27

Kangaroos 29

Aquarium 31

Animals with Long Ears 33

Cuckoo in the Woods 35

Birds 37

Pianists 39

Fossils 41

The Swan 43

Finale 44

Saint-Saëns's Carnival

Camille Saint-Saëns is a famous French composer who was born about 150 years ago. Although Saint-Saëns was a very serious composer, he also liked a good joke. That's why, when his pupils at a music school asked him to write a musical joke for them, he wrote the *Carnival of the Animals*. People enjoyed his joke so much that it has now become one of his most famous pieces of music.

Here are the animals you will meet in the music. Can you see any unusual ones?

Orchestra for the Carnival

Saint-Saëns very carefully selected the instruments to play his musical carnival. He wanted each of the animals to have its own special music. Here is the orchestra he chose, playing the *Carnival of the Animals*. The musicians are dressed up for the concert.

pianos

clarinet

flute

piccolo

baton

violins

conductor

The players sit in a half circle so that they can all see the
conductor. The conductor is in charge of the orchestra.
He waves his baton to make sure that everyone plays in time.
He tells the musicians when it is their turn to play for one of
the animals and how loudly or softly they should play.

xylophone

glockenspiel

viola

cello

double bass

String Instruments

The violin, viola, cello, and double bass are all members of the string family of instruments. The string family is the most important group of instruments in the carnival orchestra.

Each member of the string family is made of wood and has four strings. String instruments are played with a bow. The sounds are made when the bow is pulled across the strings, or when the players pluck the strings with their fingers.

bow

The violin is the smallest string instrument and it makes the highest sound. Listen for the violins playing the clucking hens and the braying donkeys.

The cello is much bigger than the violin and the viola and makes an even deeper sound. Listen to the beautiful tune it plays for the swan.

The viola looks like a big violin and has a deeper sound. It plays the tune of the fish in the aquarium.

The double bass is the biggest string instrument of all. It makes the deepest sound of all the strings. It plays a funny dance for the elephant.

Woodwind Instruments

Saint-Saëns chose three members of the woodwind family of instruments to play in his carnival. The instruments in this family are played by blowing into them, and they all have a row of holes on the top. The players make different notes by covering the holes with their fingers.

Woodwind instruments are not always made of wood. Some instruments, like the piccolo and flute, are usually made of metal—sometimes even silver or gold. Others, like the clarinet, are made of both wood and metal.

The clarinet can play loud and noisy music as well as quiet, gentle music. Listen for it playing the noisy call of the rooster as well as the gentle song of the cuckoo in the woods.

The flute is one of the highest of the woodwind instruments. It plays the fast fluttering tune of the birds.

The piccolo is the smallest woodwind instrument. It plays even higher than the flute. The piccolo plays at the end of the music when all the animals gather together for the big carnival parade.

15

Xylophone, Glockenspiel, and Piano

Saint-Saëns was a pianist, and it's not surprising that he gave the pianos a very busy part in the carnival. The piano, glockenspiel, and xylophone are all members of the important percussion family. Instruments in this family are tapped or struck to make their sounds.

Inside the piano, tiny wooden hammers strike the strings when a key is pressed. The wooden notes of the xylophone and the metal notes of the smaller glockenspiel are played with long beaters.

The xylophone makes a very rattly sound. It plays the part of the fossils.

The glockenspiel is like a small xylophone but it is made of metal. Its tinkly sound is the sunlight on the water in the aquarium.

The piano can play the highest and the lowest notes of all the instruments in the carnival orchestra. Listen as the pianos play the mad rushing music of the mule race, the bouncy kangaroo music, and the music for the noisiest animals of all—beginner pianists!

18

Royal March of the Lion

TRACK 1

Listen! The orchestra is calling our attention!
The music begins and it gets louder and louder.
Who is arriving? It's the lion! The strings are
playing the lion's marching tune as he walks
proudly around his kingdom.

Sometimes he roars loudly. Can you hear
the pianos playing the lion's roar?
Do you think the other animals are
frightened of him?

Now the music grows quiet as the lion pauses
for a moment to watch over his kingdom.
Then he roars again—one final time—
before he strides off.

Hens and Roosters

The hens' music is played by the violin and viola. They play a spiky, jumpy tune, which sounds just like hens scratching around, clucking and squawking to each other.

Can you hear the high trills on the piano? That's the rooster. "Look at me! Look at me!" he seems to cry. The rooster wants the hens to stop their clucking and admire him, but the hens take no notice.

Now the clarinet plays the part of the rooster. But you can hardly hear him above the noise, as the hens carry on scratching and clucking. Do you think the poor rooster will ever make himself heard?

Mules

Mules are slow, stubborn creatures, but these are very unusual mules. Can you hear how the music rushes up and down the piano keyboard? The mules are chasing each other! The other animals watch astonished as they rush by.

Higher and higher the music climbs. Up and up and up. And then it rushes down again, the notes almost tumbling over one another—just like the mules. Do you think it's a race? Who will finish first?

At the end of the piece we hear two loud crashes on the piano. The mules flop down exhausted. But they've had a great time.

23

Tortoises

How slowly the tortoises move . . . step . . . step . . . step. Their tune is played by the string instruments. It's a dance tune, but it's very slow and plodding. Could you dance as slowly as this?

It's as if the tortoises aren't sure which scaly foot to put next. They drag themselves along, but they don't seem to be getting anywhere. Do you think they like dancing?

The tortoises' tune gets slower and slower until it stops altogether and all you can hear is the piano. The tortoises are tired out.

The Elephant

The piano starts this piece with a waltz tune. A waltz is a gentle and graceful dance. People in Saint-Saëns's day danced the waltz at parties.

Then the double bass starts playing, all deep and gruff, plodding along next to the piano. That's the sound of the elephant trying to dance! It doesn't matter how high and fast the piano plays, the double bass just keeps on stomping steadily along.

Do you think the elephant enjoys dancing? Do you think he knows that he can't dance very well?

27

Kangaroos

Listen to the bouncy music. Here come the kangaroos. The pianos play their hopping and jumping music. It sounds as if the kangaroos themselves are leaping along the keys of a giant piano.

Sometimes the music goes very quiet as the kangaroos stand still, deciding which way to jump next. Now they're off again, jumping up the piano. Can you hear the music getting higher and higher? And then they jump all the way down again.

Very soon the kangaroos have to rest, so they stop for a long kangaroo snooze.

29

30

Aquarium

In the aquarium the rainbow colors of the fish sparkle in the sun. There are tiny fish with shiny scales and giant fish with funny faces. The flute and all the string instruments play a high, soft tune for the fish as they glide through the water.

The pianos are the gentle waves rippling across the water. At times the fish stay so still that all you can hear are the waves tripping over each other.

Listen carefully toward the end of the music. Can you hear the tinkling sound of the glockenspiel? It is the sunlight glittering on the waves, high above the fish.

Animals with Long Ears

Hee-haw! *Hee-haw!* Many animals have long ears but only one creature makes this strange sound. Do you know which animal it is? It's the donkey.

The violins play the hee-haws. First they play a loud, squeaky high note. Then they play two long low notes. *Hee-haw! Hee-haw! Hee-haw!* What a noise! What a noise! WHAT A NOISE! It gets faster and faster, louder and louder.

It's not surprising the other animals run away and cover their ears.

33

Cuckoo in the Woods

It's springtime. Deep in the woods, the air is still and warm. The cuckoo is calling.

The cuckoo's gentle call is played by the soft, sweet sound of the clarinet. The cuckoo sings only two notes—one high, one low. Can you hear which one is first?

The pianos are the noises in the woods. They play beautiful quiet music, which sounds like slow footsteps. If you follow the footsteps deeper and deeper into the woods you may actually see the cuckoo—but remember to stay very quiet and very still.

Birds

The flute plays a high fast melody as the birds flutter their wings and fly up and down, backward and forward. The music is light and bouncy. The violins hover around one note in the background, like the birds hovering in the air.

Can you hear the chirps and trills played by the pianos? They are the sounds of the birds calling to each other across the treetops.

The music grows higher and higher at the end of the piece. What do you think is happening?

Pianists

Pianists, of course, aren't really animals but these pianists want to join the carnival.

They're just beginners, so they don't play very well. Listen to them practicing their exercises. They have to play the same music over and over again. The rest of the carnival animals are tired of listening to the pianists.

The string instruments play a little tune of their own, getting faster and faster. "Hurry up and finish," they say to the pianists. "It's our turn to play now." Then, at last, the pianists stop. Hurray! All the animals are very pleased.

Fossils

It's night time, the stars are out—and the fossils are dancing in the moonlight! The bony skeletons of the dinosaurs have come alive, and the xylophone is playing their fast rattly tune.

Listen for the piano in the middle of the piece. Can you hear a well-known tune? *Twinkle, Twinkle, Little Star . . .*

At the end of the music the rest of the orchestra joins the xylophone to play the fossils' dance again. It's such a good tune, they all want to play!

41

The Swan

The music for this piece is very slow and gentle. It sounds as if the swan is gliding gracefully along a quiet river.

Can you hear the pianos in the background? They are the ripples in the water.

The main tune is played by the cello. Listen to it growing louder, and then softer. The swan is coming nearer and fluttering its wings. Then, at the end of the piece, the swan disappears into the distance, and you can only hear the sound of the water.

Finale

Now the orchestra calls all the animals
to the start of the grand carnival parade.

The pianists play great swooshing sounds, and
then the orchestra plays a special parade tune.

Suddenly, with a great clatter of hooves,
the mules rush by. Can you hear their music?

Then we hear the spiky music
of the hens and roosters.

Now the kangaroos pass by,
jumping and hopping to their tune.

Last of all we hear the loud hee-haws
of the donkeys. The animals don't cover
their ears anymore. They are
too happy and excited.

Well, it's not every day there's a
CARNIVAL OF THE ANIMALS!

45